NQA

Usborne
Illustrated
Classics
for Boys

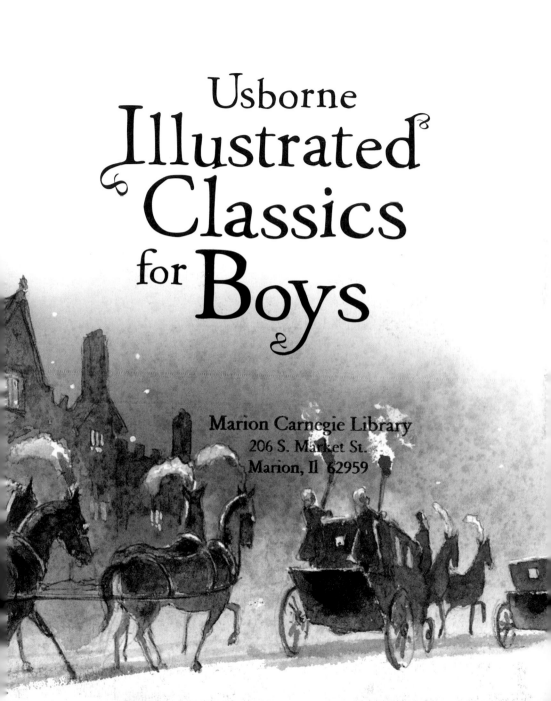

Usborne
Illustrated
Classics
for Boys

Contents

Robin Hood
7

Retold by Rob Lloyd Jones Illustrated by Alan Marks

Gulliver's Travels
71

Based on a story by Jonathan Swift
Retold by Gill Harvey Illustrated by Peter Dennis

Moonfleet
133

Based on a story by J.M. Falkner
Retold by Rob Lloyd Jones Illustrated by Alan Marks

Around the World in Eighty Days   195

Based on a story by Jules Verne
Retold by Jane Bingham Illustrated by Adam Stower

Robinson Crusoe   259

Based on a story by Daniel Defoe
Retold by Gill Harvey Illustrated by Peter Dennis

The Canterville Ghost   321

Based on a story by Oscar Wilde
Retold by Susanna Davidson Illustrated by Alan Marks

Robin Hood

The legend of Robin Hood

Tales of Robin Hood and his adventures were first told in the Middle Ages. They probably weren't written down at that time, but over the last 600 years, many books, plays and poems have been written, inspired by Robin Hood, and lots of television series and films have been made about him too. The idea of a dashing young rebel who fights the rich in order to help the poor never fails to appeal.

Chapter 1
Much Middleton

It was a sunny day in Sherwood village.
Ten-year-old Much Middleton was
helping his father in their mill.
As he lifted a sack of corn,
he heard shouting.

Dozens of soldiers pounded into the village
on horseback, led by the Sheriff of Nottingham.
"I need more money," the Sheriff declared. He
owned Sherwood and the villagers had to pay
him taxes so they could live there. "You'll
have to pay double what you paid before,"
he continued.

Much's father was furious. "Only the King is allowed to raise taxes," he protested.

The Sheriff sneered. "The King is overseas. I'm in charge now."

With that, he lashed his horse and charged back to his castle.

That evening, Much lay in bed watching his father count their money. There wasn't nearly enough. "Do you think Robin Hood could help us?" Much asked.

Robin Hood was a mysterious outlaw who stole money from the Sheriff to give to poor villagers. People said he lived in Sherwood Forest, though no one knew for sure.

Much was always asking for stories about
Robin Hood. "Is it true he once defeated twenty
of the Sheriff's men?"

"A hundred!" his father joked, waving
a shovel.

Just then, there was a noise outside.
Much's father gripped the shovel, scared
it was the Sheriff's soldiers. He flung the
door open...

...but no one was there. A silk pouch hung on the door, filled with twinkling gold coins.

Every house in the village had one.

"They're from Robin Hood," one of the villagers gasped.

"God bless him!" cried another.

"Much!" his father called. "Come quickly and see."

But Much had already seen. He sat by the window watching a shadowy figure leap across the rooftops to Sherwood Forest.

Chapter 2
On the run

The Sheriff was furious when he came back the next day. "Robin Hood stole that money from me," he spat.

Much hated the Sheriff. In a rage, he scooped up some horse dung...

...and hurled it splat into the Sheriff's face. "God bless Robin Hood!" he shouted.

Several guards tried to grab Much, but his father blocked their way. They forced his father to the ground. "Run!" he yelled to Much.

Much fled into the
forest and scrambled
up a tree to hide.
His heart was pounding.
Tears trickled down his cheeks.
His father had been arrested, and
it was all his fault.
Much was desperate to rescue
him, but how?

He needed help.
He needed to find
Robin Hood.

Chapter 3
Sherwood Forest

Much wandered deeper into the forest. The trees seemed to close in around him. He was tired, thirsty and scared.

As he stumbled along, a lone rider came down the path.

It was a woman, wearing a silk dress and a glittering necklace. "Can I give you a lift?" she asked.

Much recognized her at once – Lady Marian, the King's cousin.

"Jump up behind me," she said. "Where are you going?"

Much was exhausted. "I don't know," he mumbled, as he climbed onto Marian's horse.

Just then, Marian saw something in the trees. "Outlaws!" she cried. "Hold on tight!" She grasped the reins and they raced down the path.

Much looked up. High in the forest, several figures were leaping from tree to tree, shadowing them.

They reached a crossroads and Marian stopped the horse. "They've gone," she sighed with relief.

But she didn't see the figure reaching out behind them...

Marian screamed. Her necklace had been stolen!

Much jumped from the horse and raced into the woods. "Is that you, Robin Hood?" he shouted. "I need your help."

All he saw were the branches, rustling in the wind.

"They've gone, and taken my necklace with them," said Marian, catching up with him.

"ROBIN HOOD!" Much yelled.

At his cry, four dark figures appeared among the branches.

"You'd better come with us," one ordered. "Follow the arrows."

Thunk! An arrow thudded into the path in front of Much.

Much climbed up behind Marian again and
they followed one arrow...

then another...

then several more.

They jumped over bushes and rode under
branches, until they reached a clearing in the
heart of the forest.

Several small houses sat hidden among
a circle of trees. A tangled net of branches
disguised them from anyone who might pass.

Three men greeted the pair
with friendly smiles.
   "Are you Robin Hood?"
Much asked the
largest one.

   "No," said the
man, scratching
his bushy beard.
"I'm Little John."

"I'm Will Scarlet,"
said the little man
beside him.

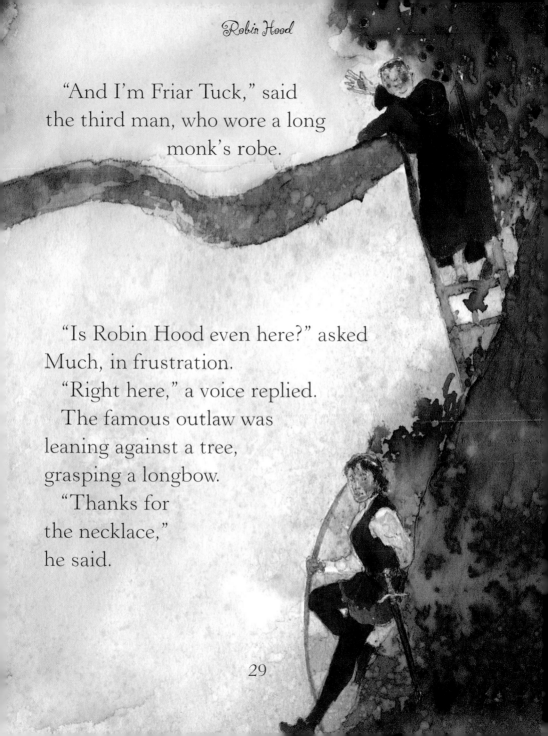

"And I'm Friar Tuck," said
the third man, who wore a long
monk's robe.

"Is Robin Hood even here?" asked
Much, in frustration.

"Right here," a voice replied.
The famous outlaw was
leaning against a tree,
grasping a longbow.

"Thanks for
the necklace,"
he said.

Marian strode forward angrily. "That necklace was a gift from my uncle," she fumed. "Why would you want it?"

"He won't keep it," Much explained. "He gives all his loot to the villagers."

"Really?" Marian asked, surprised. Robin nodded, then offered Marian her necklace back.

"In that case," Marian said, "keep it. I thought you were just a common thief."

"No," said Robin, winking at Much, "I'm a very good thief."

"We were farmers once," Robin explained, "but the Sheriff stole our land. Now, we help the villagers keep theirs."

"Can you help my father?" Much asked. "I think he's been locked in the Sheriff's dungeons."

Robin shook his head, then turned to go. "I'm sorry," he said, "that's too dangerous. The King will free him when he returns. Until then, you can live with us."

But Much was determined to rescue his father – with or without Robin Hood.

Chapter 4
Robin and Much

That night, Much stole one of the outlaw's swords and crept out of the clearing.

"Leaving already?" a voice called. Robin stepped from the shadows.

"I'm going to rescue my father," Much snapped, "because you won't."

Robin took the sword away from Much and put it down. "Come with me," he said.

Robin guided Much through the trees. They jumped from branch to branch, and swung together on tangled vines. Soon, they reached Sherwood village.

Robin handed Much a jingling pouch of coins. "Here," he said, "help me hand these out."

They split up and crept around the village, crawling across rooftops and slipping between houses to leave the money.

Much left coins on villagers' doorsteps…

on their windowsills…

…and even under their pillows. He was on a thrilling secret mission – but he couldn't forget his father.

When the money was all gone, Robin sat
down beside Much.

"This is why we can't try to rescue your
father," said Robin. "If we get caught,
how will the villagers pay
their taxes?"

Much knew Robin was right. He glared at the
Sheriff's castle. "Then, until my father is free,
I'll help you protect the villagers," he promised.

The next day, Friar Tuck cooked a huge lunch for the gang in the forest – roast deer, rabbit stew and blackberry pie.

Afterwards, Little John and Will Scarlet taught Much how to fight with a sword.

And Robin
trained him
in archery.

With each arrow,
Much got closer to
the bulls-eye...

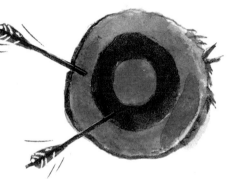

...but he was
never as good
as Robin Hood.

Much spent weeks living with Robin and his men. He helped them steal from the rich...

...and give to the poor.

He invented clever
disguises...

sneaky
hiding
places...

Thanks for
the money,
Robin Hood

...and mocking
messages for the
greedy Sheriff.

Much loved being part of Robin Hood's gang.
But he still worried about his father, locked up
in the Sheriff's castle.

Chapter 5
The Sheriff's castle

One morning, Lady Marian visited the Sheriff.
She wondered if he had any news of her cousin.
The King had been due home weeks before.

44

"My dear," the Sheriff said, "I'm afraid he is probably dead."

"And you want to replace him," Marian realized with horror.

"Who else?" boasted the Sheriff. "I'm the richest man in the country."

"You're a crook," Marian cried. "Robin Hood will stop you."

The Sheriff just sneered at the outlaw's name. "I don't think so."

The Sheriff took Marian to the next room. Six knights stood by the fire, all dressed in black. They had snake-like eyes and brutal faces.

"The Six Swordsmen," Marian gasped.

The Six Swordsmen were the most feared fighters in Europe.

"They're my new tax collectors," the
Sheriff said proudly. "I'd like to see
Robin Hood stop them."

But Marian had already gone.

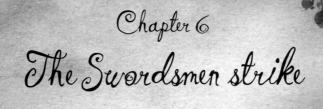

Chapter 6
The Swordsmen strike

That afternoon, while some of the outlaws took more money to the village, Robin gave Much another archery lesson. As Much pulled back his bow...

...Marian came charging into the clearing.

"Robin!" she called. "The Sheriff has hired the Six Swordsmen."

Just then, a plume of smoke rose in the sky.

"It's coming from the village!" cried Robin, grabbing his sword.

49

Much couldn't believe his eyes when they reached the village. All of the houses had been burned down, including his father's mill. The villagers wandered forlornly through the ruins.

"It was the Six Swordsmen," one said. "We gave them money, but they still destroyed our homes."

"Where are Will and Tuck and Little John?" demanded Robin.

"Captured," the villager said sadly. "The Swordsmen took them to the castle."

Robin stared up at the Sheriff's castle, his face darkening. "It's time to fight back," he declared.

"But how?" asked Marian. "The Sheriff has a whole army."

Much scrambled onto the remains of the mill and called to the villagers. "Will you join us? Will you join Robin Hood?"

"We will!" they shouted back.

Much grinned. Now they had an army too.

Chapter 7
To the castle

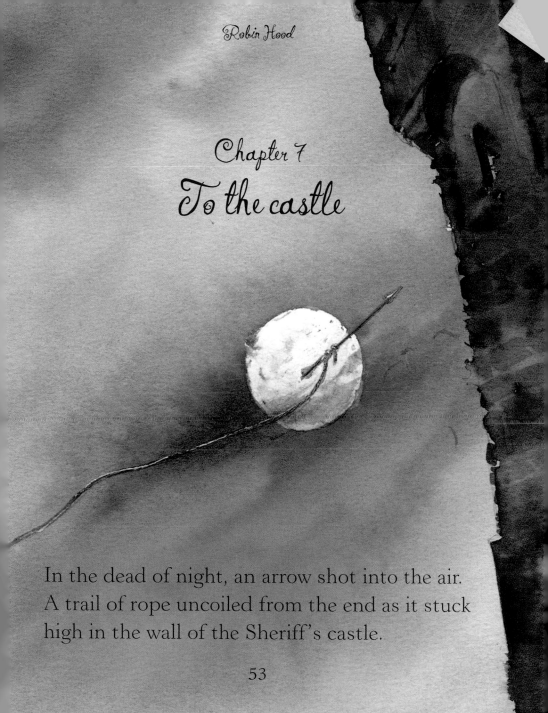

In the dead of night, an arrow shot into the air.
A trail of rope uncoiled from the end as it stuck
high in the wall of the Sheriff's castle.

Among the trees, Robin pulled the rope tight. "Are you sure you're ready?" he asked Much. Much nodded. He'd never been more sure of anything.

Below, Marian and the villagers watched in silence as the pair climbed the rope to the castle.

54

The rope dug into Much's hands.
He tried not to look down. Soon,
Robin was pulling him onto the
moonlit castle walkway. Everything
was deadly quiet...

...until a door crashed open and
the Six Swordsmen emerged.
"Robin Hood," one growled.
"We've been expecting you."

Chapter 8
Fight!

The Swordsmen charged. They were so fast,
Much could hardly see their swords. But Robin
was faster.

The outlaw twisted and twirled, ducked and dived. He drove the Swordsmen down a spiral staircase into the main hall.

Much pushed hard against a statue of the Sheriff, toppling it onto four of the Swordsmen. But there were still two left.

They lunged at Much, whirling their swords.

Much darted across the floor, but he was trapped. The Swordsmen advanced, grinning evilly. Quickly, Robin scrambled up a pillar.

Then he leaped from the balcony…

swung on the
chandelier…

…and crashed into the last two Swordsmen,
sending them flying.

"Come on!" he urged Much. "We must find
the prisoners."

But before they could move, dozens of soldiers had surrounded them, blocking the way.

The Sheriff stood by with a smug smile. "There are too many of us," he scoffed. "Even for you."

Much spun and fired a single arrow. It whizzed over their heads and through the castle entrance. At his signal, Marian and the villagers stormed inside. A huge battle began.

As the battle raged, Marian led Much down some stairs to the dungeons. There sat his father, locked in chains, alongside Little John, Will Scarlet and Friar Tuck.

They grabbed the keys from a hook and released the prisoners. Much's father scooped him up in a big hug.

When they returned to the main hall, the
fight was over. Only the Sheriff refused
to surrender.

"You can't stop me," he snarled. "The King
is dead!"

"Really?" a voice roared from the castle
entrance. "I feel quite alive."

The King strode into the hall. Marian threw her arms around him. "You're back!" she cried.

The Sheriff gave a squeal of panic, then turned and ran.

As he passed, Much stuck out a leg. The Sheriff fell screaming down the stairs to the dungeon.

Little John slammed the door, and Will Scarlet turned the key. Then they raced up the stairs and bowed to the King.

"I owe you a huge debt," the King told Robin and his men. "I'll make you all knights. You can live together in this castle."

"Thank you, sir," Robin said, "but the forest is our home."

"You can stay with us if you like," Robin added to Much.

Much shook his head. "My home is the village," he replied, hugging his father.

Robin handed Much his sword. "Keep this then, to remember us."

With that, Robin Hood and his men were gone.

"Do you think we'll ever see them again?" Much asked.

"I'm sure we will," the King replied, "if we need their help."

And so, Much Middleton's life returned to normal. The King had all of the villagers' homes rebuilt, including the mill, and Much went back to working with his father.

One thing was different, though
– now Much's father asked *him*
for stories about
Robin Hood.

Gulliver's Travels

Jonathan Swift
(1667-1745)

Jonathan Swift was born in Dublin, in Ireland. His father died before he was born and he was raised by his mother and his three uncles.

As well as writing novels and poems, he wrote dozens of essays and political pamphlets, often criticizing the way people behaved in society. *Gulliver's Travels* was his most famous novel. Published in 1726, it was an instant hit.

Chapter 1
All so small

Lemuel Gulliver loved to travel and he loved adventures. This is the story of one of his stranger adventures.

It began when Gulliver boarded a ship sailing to the Far East...

The voyage was a difficult and dangerous one. Winds howled, storms raged and the ship was pushed off course. Finally, it hit some rocks and sank.

The passengers were desperate. Some tried to escape in a small boat. But it capsized and they all drowned... except for Gulliver.

Gulliver swam for his life. Just as he was giving up hope, he saw land. He stumbled ashore and collapsed on the beach. Soon, he was fast asleep.

When he woke up, he couldn't move – not even his head. He was tied to the ground.

Gulliver tugged his hair free and looked around. An amazing sight met his eyes. Tiny men were clambering all over him. "Hey!" Gulliver shouted.

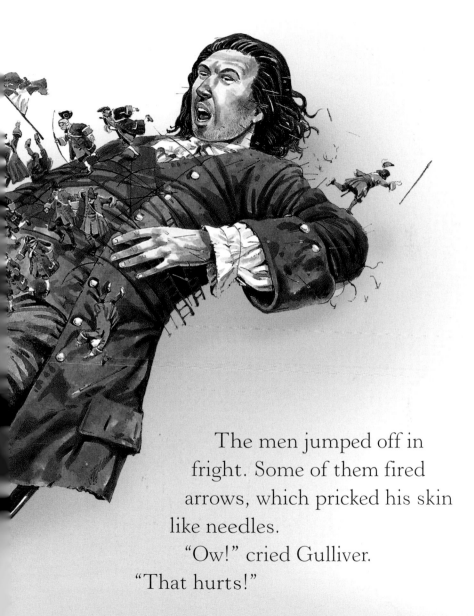

The men jumped off in
fright. Some of them fired
arrows, which pricked his skin
like needles.

"Ow!" cried Gulliver.
"That hurts!"

What were they going to do next? He soon
found out. They stopped firing arrows and built
a ladder beside him. Then an important-looking
man climbed up and shouted in his ear.

But Gulliver didn't understand a word. He
was hungry, too, so he pointed to his mouth.
"Hungry," he said.

The man must have understood him because a crowd appeared, carrying huge amounts of very small food. Gulliver gobbled it all.

Then they brought barrels of wine which Gulliver gulped down thirstily. The people gave each other sly smiles.

Unknown to Gulliver, they had put something in the wine. In seconds, he fell into a deep sleep. The people set to work.

Five hundred tiny carpenters built a wooden cart, and dragged Gulliver onto it. Then he was pulled away.

Gulliver woke up outside a magnificent temple. He was in the country's capital city, Milando. The people had brought him there because they thought it could be his new home.

After chaining his left leg to the temple, they untied the ropes that bound him to the cart.

Gulliver, who still couldn't understand them, was very confused.

As he stood there, crowds gathered to stare at him.
Gulliver was just as amazed. It was like a toy town.

Chapter 2
The emperor

As soon as the emperor of the land heard about the giant man, he came to see Gulliver. But they couldn't understand each other either.

"I need to think about this," said the emperor.
Leaving his soldiers to guard Gulliver, he
strode off.

Everyone wanted a closer look at the giant.
But some men fired more arrows at him.

"Stop that!" cried the soldiers, seizing
the men.

"Here!" one shouted. "Let's give them to the
giant to punish."

Gulliver picked up one of the troublemakers and opened his mouth. The little man wriggled and howled with terror. He was sure he was going to be eaten.

Meanwhile, the emperor was thinking hard. What should he do about Gulliver? He decided to ask his advisors.

"Let's kill him before it's too late," one of them suggested. "Anything that big MUST be dangerous."

But, as they were talking, two men arrived. They were full of news about what Gulliver had done with the men who fired arrows at him.

"He's a joker! He pretended to eat one and then he let them all go," they said, laughing.

The emperor was delighted. "Let's keep him," he said. "Give him plenty of food, make him some new clothes and teach him our language."

Soon, Gulliver had everything he needed. But he was still held in the temple, like a prisoner.

Chapter 3
Freedom

Gulliver learned the people's language as quickly as he could. Then he asked if he could see the emperor.

"Please set me free," he pleaded.

The emperor wasn't sure. "You'll have to wait," he said. "You may still be dangerous." And he sent his men to search inside Gulliver's pockets.

They found his handkerchief....

his snuff box...

his notebook...

his comb...

his watch...

and a bag
of coins.

The only dangerous thing they found was his
gun. But they didn't know what it was.

The emperor still wasn't satisfied. He sent a message to Gulliver.

"Do you have any weapons? Show them to us!" he demanded.

So Gulliver drew his sword out of its sheath, and waved it around above his head.

The emperor's troops had surrounded Gulliver at a distance, with bows and arrows ready to fire. When they saw the sword, they shouted in terror. So, Gulliver quickly put the sword down on the ground as gently as he could.

92

Then he got out his
gun and fired it into
the air. Everyone fell
to the ground in fear.

"Don't worry," Gulliver said. "You can have
them." He handed his sword and gun to the
guards and the emperor relaxed. But he still
didn't set Gulliver free.

Gulliver just had to wait. To pass the time, he learned more about the country, which was called Lilliput. It had some very strange customs.

One was the game of "Leaping and Creeping". Even important nobles played it. They had to leap over a stick or creep under one. The winners won prizes.

To work for the emperor, people had to do tricks. The top jobs went to the best acrobats.

Gulliver thought this custom was very odd, but he didn't show it. If he was friendly, they might trust him and let him go.

Every day, Gulliver begged to be allowed to leave the temple, but the emperor always refused. Then finally, one day, the emperor agreed.

"Free the giant," he declared. "He may walk where he likes. But he must ask first. And he must stay on the main roads!"

"I will!" Gulliver promised.

Free at last, Gulliver set off to explore the city. Everybody else stayed indoors, to avoid his enormous feet.

Gulliver thought he'd visit the palace, but the gate was too small and the walls were too tall.

So, he cut down some of the largest trees from the palace garden and made two stools.

With a stool on either side of the wall, he could step over into the palace courtyard.

Inside, he was taken to meet the empress and her children.

"Welcome," said the empress. She held out her hand for Gulliver to kiss.

Gulliver explored the entire city before he returned to his temple that night. When he fell asleep, he had a smile on his face.

Chapter 4
War!

Lilliput seemed like a very peaceful place but Gulliver soon found out that it wasn't. One day, the emperor's secretary came to see him.

"We have a problem," he said. "There are two groups of people in Lilliput. The Tramecksans wear high heels and the Slamecksans wear low ones. They're bitter enemies and both groups want to be in charge."

"The emperor likes low heels at the moment, so the Slamecksans have more power. But if he changes his mind, war could break out!"

"That's terrible!" said Gulliver.

"And that's not all!" cried the secretary.
"We're already at war, with a nearby island
called Blefescu – and the islanders are going to
attack us!"

"Why do they want to attack you?" asked
Gulliver. "What's the problem between you?"

"It's all about eggs," explained the secretary. "Boiled eggs and a cut finger."

Gulliver was astonished. "Eggs!" he said. "How?"

The secretary blushed. "Well, many years ago, everyone opened their eggs at the big end. But then the prince cut his finger when breaking his egg open."

"His father passed a law at once. No one was to crack their eggs at the big end, ever again. Eggs always had to be eaten from the smaller end."

"Lots of people refused to obey the law. They were ready to die over it and some were killed.

But others fled to Blefescu, because there people still cracked their eggs at the big end."

"We've been at war ever since. We've already lost forty ships, and thousands of our soldiers and sailors have died. And now, the Blefescudians have built a huge fleet of ships and they are preparing to invade Lilliput. You have to help us," the secretary pleaded. "Please!"

Gulliver listened carefully to the sad tale. "I'll do everything I can to protect the emperor and Lilliput," he promised.

He tried to find the island of Blefescu with his telescope. It was easy to spot. A fleet of ships was getting ready to set out. Gulliver counted over fifty warships.

But what could he do on his own against so many warships?

Suddenly, he had an idea...

"I'll need ropes and iron bars," he told
the emperor.

Gulliver twisted the ropes together to make
them stronger. Then he bent the iron bars
into hooks.

"Now for the next stage of my plan," he muttered, heading to the sea. Gulliver waded in and swam almost all the way to Blefescu.

When he rose out of the sea, towering above them, the sailors screamed with fright. Many dived overboard, just to escape.

Gulliver hooked a rope to each of the ships and tied the ropes together. Then he hauled the fleet back across the sea to Lilliput.

Chapter 5
Gulliver in danger

When Gulliver arrived at Lilliput's shores, everyone cheered. But defeating Blefescu's navy wasn't enough for the emperor.

"I want to take over Blefescu," he announced to Gulliver.

Gulliver thought that was going too far. "I won't make people into slaves," he said.

This made the emperor cross. Then some messengers arrived from Blefescu, hoping to make peace. When they met Gulliver, they invited him for a visit.

This made the emperor furious. "Hrmph," he said, crossly. "I suppose you can go. If you must."

Gulliver thought he'd better stay in Lilliput and try to keep the emperor happy.

He stayed quietly in his temple until, one night, he was woken by shouting.
"HELP! HELP! Gulliver! Come quickly! The palace is on fire!"

People were frantically fighting the fire, but flames were licking the roof. Gulliver, who was taller than the tallest ladder, threw water over the palace to save it.

After this, the emperor was happy again for a while. Gulliver began to enjoy life, although he kept thinking of home. But most people were very kind to him.

Three hundred tailors made him a new blue suit, and, every day, three hundred chefs cooked him tasty meals.

One evening, the emperor even brought his family to visit Gulliver. They all sat down to a wonderful feast at Gulliver's table.

But Gulliver's problems didn't go away. Flimnap, who was in charge of the emperor's money, didn't like Gulliver. He said he cost too much.

"Your highness, he eats far too much," Flimnap complained.

"I suppose you've got a point," the emperor nodded thoughtfully. It was true. Gulliver was very expensive.

Late one night, Gulliver had a visitor – an important noble from the palace, who kept his face hidden.

He had come with a warning.

"Listen carefully! Your life's in danger. Flimnap is turning everyone against you," he told Gulliver.

"Your enemies have written a list of your crimes. They say you can't be trusted – that you're a traitor," he said.

"Even worse, they say you're plotting against the emperor. They want you killed."

"Flimnap wants to set your temple on fire and shoot poisoned arrows at you!"

Gulliver turned pale.

"Not all of the nobles want to kill you," the man added. "Some say you should only be blinded."

"But even the emperor wants to give you less food, to save money. You must leave. Right away!"

Chapter 6
Escape plans

Gulliver didn't waste any time. Quickly, he scribbled a letter to the emperor.

"I'm off to visit Blefescu, as I promised," he wrote.

Then he hurried down to the sea and undressed. He piled his clothes onto the biggest ship he could find and waded into the sea between Lilliput and Blefescu.

Gulliver didn't stop until he had reached Blefescu. The king himself came out to meet him. Gulliver lay down to kiss his hand.

"Welcome!" cried the king. "Stay as long as you like."

"I'm very grateful, your majesty," Gulliver replied truthfully.

Walking on the beach a week later, Gulliver spotted something strange out at sea.

It was a small boat – but a full-sized one – floating upside down in the water.

Gulliver rushed to the king. "Please help me!" he begged.

"This could be my chance to go home. Can you help me rescue the boat?"

"Of course," said the king. "Take some ships to help you."

Gulliver swam out to the boat, holding ropes from each of the ships.

With the ships pulling and Gulliver pushing, the boat was brought safely to shore.

Gulliver set about fixing the boat for his long journey home. While he carved a tree trunk to make a mast, some of the king's men made a new sail.

The sail was like a quilt, made of thirteen layers of the strongest fabric in the land.

Soon, the boat was finished. "I'd like to leave now," Gulliver told the king. "But no one at home will believe my story. Could I take some of your people with me?"

"I think your people would enjoy seeing my country," he added.

"I can't possibly allow that," said the king. "But you may take some cows and a sheep or two."

He also gave Gulliver fifty bags of gold coins. "I don't want you to go," he said. "But I understand why you have to."

"Thank you," said Gulliver. "I'll never forget you all."

He clambered into his boat and set sail. "Goodbye, Blefescu!" he cried. "Goodbye!"

After only a few days at sea, Gulliver saw a ship. He shouted and waved wildly, hoping the sailors would see him.

He was in luck! The lookout spotted him. The ship sailed over and picked him up.

"Where have you come from?" asked the captain.

"A place called Lilliput," said Gulliver and he showed the captain his souvenirs.

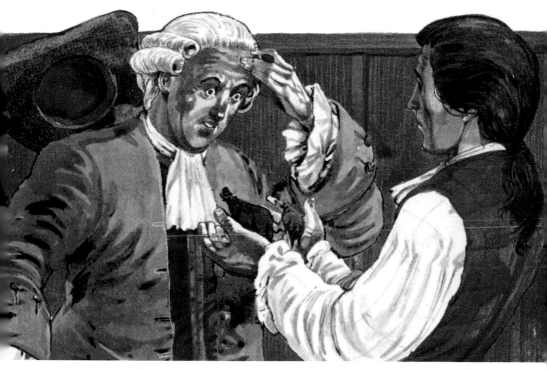

The captain was astonished. For a few gold coins and a couple of cows, he agreed to take Gulliver all the way home.

Moonfleet

John Meade Falkner (1858-1932)

John Meade Falkner was born in Wiltshire, England. After attending university, he became a teacher, then a private tutor, and later a business man.

He wrote *Moonfleet*, an action-filled tale of smuggling and adventure, in 1898, basing the village of Moonfleet on East Fleet, a fishing village in Dorset on the south coast of England.

He set his story in the middle of the 18th century, when smugglers lurked around the south coast of England. These were men who hid goods brought from other countries, so they didn't have to pay taxes on them. Government officials, known as magistrates, did everything they could to stop the smugglers – even if that meant killing them.

Chapter 1
Moonfleet village

My name is John Trenchard, and I was
fifteen years old when this story began, on a
stormy night in Moonfleet village.

Fierce winds swept from the sea, shaking our
houses, shattering windows, and sending tiles
flying from roofs. In the bay, huge waves broke
over the cliffs, flooding the cobbled streets.

   The next morning, we had to tiptoe through
mud as the church bells called us to the Sunday
service. We all sat wrapped up in thick coats as
Mr. Glennie, the minister, began his sermon.
Suddenly, a strange noise echoed around the
walls – a knocking sound, like boats jostling at
sea. Everyone jumped up, listening to the eerie
noises. They were coming from the vault under
the church.

"It's Blackbeard!" someone shouted. Everyone shuddered. Blackbeard was the nickname of John Mohune, a rich noble who owned the village over a hundred years ago. His tomb sat beneath the church, but many villagers believed his ghost still haunted Moonfleet, protecting treasure he had buried before he died.

Mr. Glennie just laughed. "The noises aren't ghosts," he said. "The floods have filled the vault with water, and the sounds are coffins banging against each other as they float."

Still, I wasn't convinced. The coffins in the vault were a hundred years old, and would surely be rotten by now. The noises we'd heard sounded like solid wood.

After the service I crept outside to investigate. Usually, the heavy stone entrance to the vault was sealed shut, but the floods had forced it open. To my amazement, I could see a dark tunnel leading under the church.

All I could think about was Blackbeard's treasure. Could it be hidden inside his vault? I was desperate to find out. But I would have to go home for a candle and, anyway, I was late for lunch. I decided to return later to hunt for the treasure.

Chapter 2
The secret vault

Back home, Aunt Jane greeted me with a
scowl. "You're late John," she snapped.
"Your lunch is cold now."

My parents had died when I was very young,
and I had lived with my aunt ever since. She
was a stern woman, who rarely allowed me out
of the house. So, that night, I waited until I
heard her snoring in her room, then grabbed a
candle and slipped out in secret.

I was so excited about the treasure, I didn't even feel scared until I reached the churchyard. Then I remembered the noises from beneath the church, and the stories of Blackbeard's ghost. But the lure of treasure drew me on, and soon I was back at the entrance to Blackbeard's vault.

I lit the candle and stepped inside. My heart was pounding as I followed a tunnel to a set of steps that curved under the church. At the bottom lay a dark chamber.

Inside, several old coffins lay on shelves
around the walls. But the floor of the vault was
filled with brand new barrels. To my horror, I
realized I had discovered a smugglers' hideout.
It must have been these barrels that had made
the noises we heard in church.

I had to get out – smugglers were dangerous
men, who didn't look kindly on spying eyes.
But, as I turned to go, I heard a voice in the
tunnel. Someone was coming!

I quickly snuffed out my candle, and hid behind a coffin as two men entered the vault and set down some more barrels. Peeking over the edge, I saw that one of them was the church groundskeeper, Ratsey, and the other was Elzivir Block, who owned a local inn called the *Why Not*. Last year, his son David had been shot and killed by Maskew, a local magistrate who had caught him smuggling.

Eventually, the smugglers left and I climbed from my hiding place. Dizzy from the stale vault air, I slipped and knocked the lid from a coffin. Inside, a body lay wrapped in cloth. Part of it was torn, and I could see bushy black hair around the figure's neck. I was sure it was Blackbeard. Could his treasure be inside the coffin?

With trembling hands, I relit the candle. A silver locket hung around Blackbeard's neck. I lifted it away, hoping to find some jewels inside, but all it held was a scrap of paper with what seemed to be a prayer written on it.

Disappointed, I looped the locket around my neck and returned along the tunnel. But now I discovered the entrance had been sealed. The smugglers must have covered it when they left. I pushed at the stone blocking my way out, but I couldn't shift it.

Now I realized why I had felt dizzy – there was no air here underground. Crazy with panic, I bashed at the door, screaming for help. But it was no good. My candle burned out. Everything went dark and I fell to the floor.

Chapter 3

Elzivir Block

I woke to find myself lying in bed. At first I thought that everything had been a dream, but then I felt the locket around my neck and knew I had been rescued.

The door creaked open, and Elzivir Block came in. I thought he would be furious that I had found his smugglers' den, but instead he smiled and handed me a bowl of soup. As I drank it, he told me how he and Ratsey had heard my shouts from the vault. They had raced back and found me lying unconscious inside. I was now upstairs in Elzivir's inn, the *Why Not*.

"You can stay here until you're well again," Elzivir said.

I stayed in bed for several days. All the time, Elzivir looked after me like a nurse. I had always thought he was stern and fierce, but I have never known anyone kinder than he was then.

Elzivir had already told my aunt where I was, but when I finally returned to her house, she refused to let me in. "You chose to run away," she snapped, "so now you can stay away."

I was homeless. The only friend I had was Elzivir, so I returned to the *Why Not* and told him what had happened.

"You must live here then," he said. "There's plenty of room."

So, I began to live with Elzivir at the old tavern. In the mornings I went to school, but I spent my afternoons helping him in the gardens or with his boats in the bay. Elzivir had lived alone since his son died, and I think he was glad for the company. He rarely mentioned David, but spoke often about his hatred for Mr. Maskew, the magistrate who killed him.

One afternoon, I was walking in the woods when I met Maskew's daughter, Grace. I knew Grace Maskew from school. She was pretty and kind and I had always liked her. As we walked together, I couldn't help telling her everything that had happened. Grace looked worried.

"John," she said, "please be careful."

I knew what Grace meant. Elzivir was a smuggler, and now that I was living with him, she thought I might become one myself. Grace's father hated smugglers, and was determined to rid Moonfleet of them all. One evening, I discovered just how determined he was.

Elzivir and I were playing cards
in the *Why Not*, when the magistrate
burst through the door. Elzivir leapt up, his
face red with rage. "You're not welcome in my
house," he cried.

149

"Your house?" Maskew said, "Not for long!" and he threw a piece of paper onto the bar.

Elzivir read it in silence, then handed it to me. It was about the *Why Not*. He had never owned the tavern, but rented it from a local landlord. Now Maskew had offered the landlord more money than Elzivir to buy it for himself.

"I want you both out by next week," he said, slamming the door as he left.

"Elzivir," I cried, "what will we do? We don't have enough money to keep the *Why Not*."

"There is one way," Elzivir replied. "A smugglers' ship is bringing a new cargo into Hoar Head Bay tomorrow night. It's a heavy load, and the job will pay well for the men who help carry it ashore. Will you join us?"

Smuggling! The thought terrified me, but Elzivir had been so kind, I was determined not to let him down. "I will," I said.

That night, I met Grace in the woods, and told her the news. She was still worried about the danger of smuggling, and scared I might get caught.

"It's only once," I promised her, "and when I return, I'll have made my own money."

"Then I'll keep a candle burning in my window until you do," she said.

Chapter 4
Hoar Head Bay

It was midnight when Elzivir and I reached Hoar Head Bay. Several other smugglers were already on the beach, hiding in the shadows by the cliff. Seeing that I was with Elzivir, they greeted me as a friend.

"The ship should arrive soon," they told me. "Wait with us."

Several hours passed. I sat beside some rocks, at first fidgeting with nerves.

At last, there came a shout. "The ship," someone yelled. "It's here!"

152

Everyone rushed to pull the ship up onto the pebbly beach. Heavy barrels, filled with brandy, were passed down from the deck and packed into carts. Soon they were all unloaded, and the ship was heading back out to sea. Just then, one of the smugglers spotted a figure hiding among some rocks. "Over there," he cried. "A spy!"

Several of the smugglers chased off after the figure. A few minutes later, they returned dragging a prisoner – Mr. Maskew!

"Shoot him," someone said.

"Don't touch him," Elzivir shouted. "Leave him with me, and go your ways."

Everyone knew that Maskew had killed Elzivir's son. Now was his chance for revenge. Taking the barrels, the other smugglers left us alone with our prisoner.

Elzivir raised a pistol to the magistrate's head. His hand shook with rage.

"Spare me, Mr. Block," Maskew grovelled. "Oh, spare me please!"

"Elzivir," I pleaded. "Don't shoot!" I hated Maskew too, but I couldn't let Elzivir kill him – he was Grace's father.

Elzivir looked at me, and I saw his pistol lower. Then a shout came from above.

"Stop! In the name of the King!" Dozens of soldiers appeared at the top of the cliff.

"Over here," Maskew yelled. "Save me!"

The soldiers raised their rifles and fired. Elzivir and I dived away, but the bullets tore into Mr. Maskew, killing him instantly.

"Run for the cliffs," Elzivir shouted.

I began to run, but the soldiers fired again and a bullet hit my leg. Elzivir rushed over and lifted me up. The pain was incredible.

"I'm sorry, John," he said, "but the soldiers will think we killed Maskew. If they catch us, we will hang for sure."

155

The only escape was a narrow path that zig-zagged up the steep side of a cliff. Below us was a huge drop, but Elzivir never slipped and never let me fall. When we reached the top, I lay on the soft grass, gasping with pain.

"We must keep moving, lad," Elzivir said. "Those soldiers will find a way up soon enough."

Elzivir lifted me onto his back and we continued, crossing fields and streams, until we reached an old stone quarry and the entrance to a cave.

Elzivir gave me some water to drink and made a fire. "We can hide here until your leg is healed," he said. "Then we must find passage overseas on a smuggling ship."

Several weeks passed as I recovered. Elzivir cleaned the wound each day and talked to me to keep my mind off the pain. He had to risk leaving the cave to find us food, and was sometimes gone for several days at a time.

Alone at night, the cave terrified me. The wind screamed through the entrance, and the fire cast eerie shadows around the walls. I sat clutching the locket I had stolen from Blackbeard's coffin, and read the prayer written inside. I hoped it would guard me against evil spirits.

Then, one night, I noticed something strange about the writing. Four of the words were written in darker ink than the others.

From eight to **eighty** I shall trek
Until my **feet** are tired and worn
But as I walk **down** life's hard road
God's love will keep me **well** and warm

As I stared at the words, my thoughts returned to Blackbeard's treasure. Was this a code to reveal its hiding place? When I showed Elzivir, his eyes lit up.

"John," he said, "before Blackbeard came to Moonfleet, he lived in Carisbrook Castle. The castle is a prison now, but I have heard that there is a deep well inside!"

"Elzivir," I cried, "the treasure must be hidden in that well – eighty feet down."

Chapter 5
The well

Dark clouds rumbled over Carisbrook Castle as we approached. Elzivir rang a bell beside the huge iron gate. Moments later, it creaked open and the prison guard grinned at us with dirty brown teeth. We had met him in secret the night before, and he'd agreed to take us to the prison's well in exchange for a share of the treasure. He had a shifty look about him that I didn't trust, but we had no choice. "Come on," he snarled. "Hurry up!"

We followed him along a dark corridor, and I heard prisoners moaning inside their cells. The guard unlocked one of the old doors and heaved it open. Inside, a barred window let in enough light to see a dark hole in the floor, with a dirty bucket hanging above it on a rope. I peered into the grimy pit, remembering Blackbeard's message – eighty feet down. Below, the murky darkness seemed to go on forever.

"There's the well," the guard said. "Now, where's this treasure?"

"We think it's in this well," I said. "I'm the lightest, so why don't you both lower me down in the bucket? If you stop when you've let out eighty feet of rope, I should be in the right place."

"John," Elzivir whispered, "be careful. I have already lost my son. I would rather lose all the treasure in the world than lose you too."

I climbed into the bucket, and Elzivir and the guard lowered me into the dreadful depths. Above, the hole grew smaller and smaller.

"John," Elzivir shouted finally, "you're eighty feet deep now."

Raising the guard's lamp, I looked around. The bricks were mossy and worn with age. But I noticed that one of them was not as old as the others. My heart raced – had I found it? I carefully pulled the brick from the wall. Behind it was a small gap... and in it sat a tiny bag. My fingers trembled as I pulled it out and peered inside.

"Have you found anything?" the guard shouted.

Inside the bag was a huge diamond, the size of a walnut.

"Yes," I shouted, "I've found the treasure! Pull me up!"

As soon as I reached the top, I jumped from the bucket, holding up the bag triumphantly. Then I froze – the guard was pointing a pistol right at me.

"Give me the treasure," he growled, "or I'll kill you."

Suddenly, Elzivir leapt at him and they fell into a savage fight. The guard was bigger than Elzivir, but not as strong. Just as he charged again, Elzivir flipped him over his shoulder. I heard a terrible scream as the guard plunged into the well and fell to his death.

"Quickly John," Elzivir cried, "another guard might come."

The prison gates slammed shut behind us as we raced away with the treasure.

Chapter 6
The diamond dealer

That night, Elzivir arranged for a ship to take us to The Hague, a city in Holland. He had heard that it was a good place to sell jewels. I sat on deck, holding the diamond and watching it sparkle in the moonlight. Elzivir stared at the stone too, but he looked worried.

"John," he said, "ever since you first looked for that treasure, luck has run against you. I think that diamond is cursed."

But I didn't listen. Instead, I thought about how I would return to Moonfleet a rich man and marry Grace.

In The Hague, we learned that the richest diamond dealer, a man named Mr. Aldobrand, lived in a huge white mansion on the outskirts of the town. I knocked on the door, and an old man with wrinkled skin answered.

"Are you Mr. Aldobrand?" I asked. "We've come all the way from Moonfleet with a diamond to sell."

The old man plucked the jewel from my hand, and studied it for a long moment.

"Come in then," he said finally.

Mr. Aldobrand led us along a hallway, where several guards sat watching us suspiciously.

"Don't worry about them," Mr. Aldobrand muttered, "they're just for security."

He guided us into a study filled with dusty books. The sun was just setting and its red light fell through the large bay windows. Mr. Aldobrand sat at a desk inspecting the diamond with a magnifying glass as I fidgeted with suspense.

"Well," I asked, "how much is it worth?"

"Nothing," Mr. Aldobrand said. "I am sorry, but this diamond is a fake. It's glass."

"Fake?" I said. "That's not possible!"

"I assure you it is," he replied. "But I will still pay you ten pounds for it."

Elzivir snatched the jewel from the desk.
"We did not come here for pennies," he cried.
"I am glad to be rid of the thing!" And he
hurled the diamond out of the window.

I watched in horror as the jewel landed in a
flowerbed outside. Elzivir stormed off, but as
I went to follow him, I caught Mr. Aldobrand
looking to see where the diamond landed too.

Outside, I told Elzivir what I had seen.

"I don't think the diamond is fake at all," I said. "Mr. Aldobrand was lying to buy it cheaply. We have to find it before he does."

Elzivir gripped my shoulders and looked me in the eye. I had never seen him so serious. "John," he said, "that diamond is cursed. Let it be."

How desperately I wish that I had listened to him, but instead I crept off down the side of the house, and climbed a wall into Mr. Aldobrand's garden.

Elzivir followed in silence.

It was darker now, though there was still enough moonlight to look for the diamond. But when I reached the flowerbed where it had landed, the jewel was gone.

"Elzivir," I whispered. "Mr. Aldobrand has already taken it."

"Then let us go home," Elzivir pleaded.

"No," I said. "He must have it inside the house."

Before Elzivir could stop me, I ran to the back of the house and peeked through a gap in the curtains. Inside, Mr. Aldobrand sat at his desk. He had a self-satisfied grin on his face... and our diamond in his hand.

Rage built up inside me. I hurled myself
forward, smashing through the window and into
the study.

"Thieves!" Mr. Aldobrand screeched. "Help!"

I grabbed the diamond from him, but the
door crashed open and Aldobrand's guards
charged in carrying clubs. Three of them
attacked Elzivir, and two came for me, raining
blows on us with sticks and fists. The last thing
I saw was the diamond falling to the floor, and
then I did the same.

Chapter 7
Prisoners

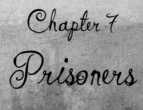

Elzivir and I were thrown into a cold
prison cell and left in the dark. I slumped in a
corner, aching from the blows from the
guards' clubs.

Several days later, the door burst open and
guards marched us to a courthouse. There, Mr.
Aldobrand told the judge that we had broken
into his house to steal his diamond.

"Liar!" I shouted, but a guard struck me on
the head.

"You are both greedy thieves," the judge said, "and I sentence you to work on a chain gang – for the rest of your lives."

As the guards led us away, I leaned over to Mr. Aldobrand. "Now you have the treasure," I told him, "and may it curse you the way it has me."

Elzivir and I were shackled in irons and
marched with hundreds of other criminals to
a place called Ymeguen, where we were made
to build a new fortress. Guards stood by with
whips and guns as we toiled in the blistering
summer sun.

Elzivir was put to work on a different part
of the building, so I barely saw him any more.
Instead, I worked alone, thinking about the
pain I had caused him, and how much I missed
Grace back in Moonfleet.

Ten years later, when I was 26, the fortress was finally finished. One morning, the guards handed some of us over to soldiers, who led us onto a ship at a nearby dock. "Please, where are we going?" I begged one of them.

"Java," he laughed, and lashed me with his whip.

My heart broke. Java was a slave colony on the other side of the world. No prisoner who went there ever returned.

The guards shoved us onto the ship and into a tiny room below deck. Another group of prisoners was already down there, crammed in like pigs in a pen. As my eyes adjusted to the dark, I thought I saw a familiar face. It was Elzivir! His hair was turning white, and his body looked old and tired, but he still found a smile for me.

"I am sorry Elzivir," I cried, hugging him. "I am so sorry."

After that, there was little to say. We were
sailing to become slaves on the other side of the
world. All hope was gone of ever seeing Grace,
Moonfleet or freedom again.

The journey was terrible. There was little light
or air below deck and, as the sea grew rougher,
many of the prisoners became badly seasick. A
week passed, and the weather grew worse. The
ship rolled violently over the waves, tossing
us about. Then, one night, the hatch above us
opened and a guard peered down. His face was
white with fear.

"Abandon ship,"
he cried. "We're
sinking!"

Chapter 8
Shipwreck

Elzivir and I scrambled up to the deck. All around us, waves rose up like mountains. The guards had gone – and taken all the lifeboats with them.

"They've left us to die like rats," Elzivir spat. But now I saw something else. There, in the distance, was a line of cliffs.

"Elzivir," I shouted, "those cliffs… We're in Moonfleet Bay!"

Elzivir spotted the cliffs too and a brief smile
flashed across his face. Battling against the
crashing waves, he climbed up to the ship's
steering wheel. "We're not safe yet," he cried,
"I'll try to turn us inland."

There were rocks everywhere and the storm
was getting worse. The other prisoners were
wild with fear. But, gradually, the ship began
to turn.

"John," Elzivir shouted, "look!" He pointed
to a small light, flickering on the cliff top. My
heart soared. Grace said she would
burn a candle until I returned.
Had she waited all this time?

We drew closer and closer to the shore. But then I heard a deafening crash.

"We've hit the rocks," Elzivir shouted. The ship flipped on its side, throwing us all headlong into the sea. Waves hammered down on us. I could see villagers calling from the beach, desperate to help. We had little chance of swimming that far, but we had to try.

We swam for our lives. I saw the villagers throwing a rope for us to catch, then Elzivir grabbing it. He reached out for me, but I heard a thunder from behind and another great wave smashed me to the shallow seabed.

I thought I was going to die, but then someone dragged me back to the surface.

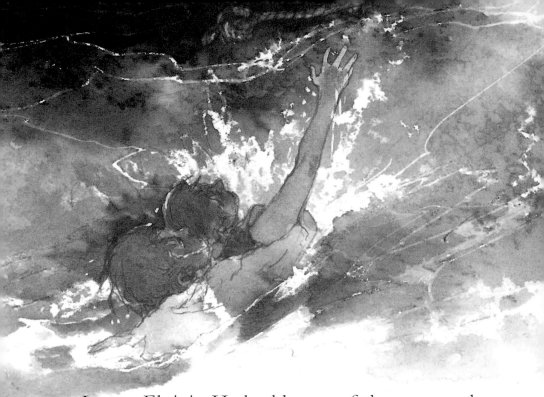

It was Elzivir. He had let go of the rope and swum back to save me. Elzivir pulled me through the waves, swimming for the shore. "The rope," he shouted, "grab the rope, John!"

The villagers' rope was an arm's length away. Just as another wave came, Elzivir shoved me forward with all his might. There was a roar of water and I caught the rope. I felt the line pull, and in seconds I was lying safe on the beach.

I looked for Elzivir, but the wave had dragged him back out to sea. I tried to call his name, but I was numb with cold.

Tears poured down my cheeks as I stared out at the crashing waves. Elzivir had drowned. He had given up his life, here on Moonfleet beach, for me.

Chapter 9
The letter

Morning was breaking as I walked up through
Moonfleet village. The storm had died and
clouds had given way to a brilliant blue sky. The
village looked the same as it had years ago.

There was my aunt's house, the church, and
the *Why Not* inn. I entered the old tavern, and
found it cobwebbed and empty. I lit a fire,
then sat with my head in my hands, crying
for Elzivir.

After a while, I felt a light touch on my shoulder. "John," a voice said, "I kept a candle burning for you. But have you forgotten me?"

It was Grace, grown up and more beautiful than ever. She sat with me, and I told her everything that had happened since I last left Moonfleet. "Grace," I said, "I am a broken wretch, with no money."

Grace just smiled and took my hand. "John," she replied, "it is not money that makes a man. Elzivir was right. That treasure was cursed. And if you ever find it again, you must use it to help others."

I was about to ask her what she meant, when Ratsey came in with Mr. Glennie, the minister. Both had grown old, but I recognized them immediately. I told Ratsey how Elzivir had died, and saw tears in his eyes. Then Mr. Glennie unfolded an old letter.

"John, do you know someone named Mr. Aldobrand?" he asked.

"Only too well," I replied, startled. I told them about the old diamond dealer, and how he had lied to send Elzivir and me to slavery.

"Well," Mr. Glennie said, "this letter is from him. It arrived here eight years ago. After you last saw him, his business collapsed. His health failed too, and he told people you had put a curse on him in court."

I remembered my words in the courthouse.
Now you have the treasure, and may it curse you the way it has me.

"But what have his fortunes to do with me?"
I asked.

"Before he died," Mr. Glennie continued,
"Mr. Aldobrand lost all of his wealth except the
money your diamond brought him. He left that
money for you, hoping it would free him from
the curse."

And so all of that great fortune became mine. But I never kept a penny for myself. Instead, we gave some to old sailors who needed it the most, and the rest was used to build a new lighthouse above Moonfleet Bay.

I married Grace, and we spent
our days walking in the woods, as we
had years ago. I am older now, and happy.
But I will never forget Elzivir. On stormy nights,
I sit and watch the waves crash over Moonfleet
Bay and remember the night that my friend
saved me.

Around the World in Eighty Days

Jules Verne (1828-1905)

Jules Verne was a French writer who loved science and travel.
He combined them with adventure in his stories.
His first book, *Five Weeks in a Balloon*, was published in
1863. Ten years later, he wrote *Around the World in Eighty
Days*. Another of his famous stories is *Twenty Thousand
Leagues Under the Sea*.

Chapter 1
The journey begins

Over one hundred years ago, there lived a man named Phileas Fogg. For many years, he led a very quiet life. He spent every day at his club, which was where rich men went to meet their friends.

Every morning, he left his house at exactly 11:30 and walked 576 steps to his club. Then he ate lunch.

After lunch, Fogg read three newspapers from cover to cover. Then he ate supper. After that, he played cards with friends. He won most of the rounds.

On the stroke of midnight, he went home to bed... before doing exactly the same the very next day.

But one Wednesday, everything changed. Fogg read some amazing news in his paper.

"Listen to this," he announced to his friends. "It says it's possible to travel around the world in only eighty days!"

"Surely not!" one of his friends declared.

"I'd like to see *you* do it!" said the other.

Despite his friends' laughter, Fogg was convinced he *could* do it.

"I will bet twenty thousand pounds that I can go around the world in eighty days or less!"

Everyone thought he was crazy, but Fogg had made up his mind.

"I shall be back on December 21st," he declared confidently, turning to leave.

As soon as he arrived home, Fogg asked Passepartout, his butler, to pack a small bag. Luckily, Passepartout had been an acrobat and could move quickly.

In less than ten minutes, they were on their way to the station...

...and at 8:45 exactly, the train pulled out. Fogg and Passepartout were off on their great adventure.

They were heading for the coast, where they could catch a boat to France. But they were also heading straight for trouble.

Chapter 2
Arriving in Africa

While Phileas Fogg was crossing Europe, the police were hunting a runaway thief. Only a few days before, he had stolen the huge sum of fifty-five thousand pounds from the Bank of England.

An inspector named Fix was convinced the thief would escape by sailing from Europe to Africa. He was waiting on the quay when Fogg reached Suez in North Africa.

Fogg sent Passepartout to get his passport stamped. "I need proof of the trip," he explained.

Quite by chance, Passepartout happened to ask Inspector Fix which was the way to the passport office.

When Fix saw the passport, he gasped. Fogg's description exactly matched the description of the thief. Fix was certain he'd found his man.

But he couldn't act at once. First, he needed some papers, which would allow him to arrest the thief.

So, Fix found out where Fogg was going and sent an urgent message to London. "Am on the trail of the thief. Following him to India. Send arrest papers to Bombay."

Fix quickly packed a small bag and boarded the ship for India.

The voyage was rough, but Fogg stayed as
calm as ever. He ate four meals a day and played
cards. He might have been at home.

Two days early, the ship steamed into
Bombay. Inspector Fix was ready to make his
arrest, but the papers had not arrived.

"My only hope," Fix decided, "is to stop
Fogg from leaving India." Later that day, he saw
his chance.

Passepartout had visited a temple, but he didn't realize he was supposed to take off his shoes. When a priest tugged them from his feet, he started a fight.

Fix was delighted. "Now I've seen that butler break the law, I can make sure he's arrested and jailed here – along with his master!"

Fix followed Passepartout to the station and watched him catch a train. "See you in Calcutta," Fix muttered to himself. "I'll get your Mr. Fogg there."

Chapter 3
Fogg to the rescue

The train puffed its way through India, passing
magnificent temples and fields of coffee and
cotton. Passepartout saw it all, amazed. Fogg
found a man to play cards.

But halfway through the third day, the train came to a stop.

"The track ends here," a guard announced. "It starts again in fifty miles at Allahabad."

Passepartout was furious. "How will we reach Calcutta in time?" he demanded.

212

Fogg didn't seem worried. "I've allowed time for delays," he said quietly. "We simply need to find another way to travel."

Passepartout rushed off. Soon, he was back with the answer

— an elephant.

The elephant was expensive, but Fogg didn't mind. He invited his card-playing friend to join them.

Then he hired a guide and, half an hour later, they were lurching through the jungle. Passepartout bounced up and down with glee. Every now and then, he tossed the elephant a sugar lump.

They journeyed for hours, crossing forests of date trees and sandy plains. That night, they camped in a ruined bungalow.

They were off again at six the next morning, breakfasting on bananas picked from a tree. They had almost crossed a thick forest, when they heard music and voices. A large procession was snaking its way through the trees.

In the middle of the procession, a group of warriors carried the body of a dead prince. Behind them, two priests were pulling a beautiful girl.

Passepartout was shocked. "What are they doing?" he cried.

"It's the custom," their guide explained. "When a prince dies, his wife must die too, so they can go to heaven together."

"Tomorrow, Princess Aouda will be burned to death beside her husband."

Passepartout was horrified. Even Phileas Fogg, who let nothing disturb him, seemed upset.

"I have twelve hours to spare," he observed. "Let's save her."

By nightfall, the procession had reached a small temple. The princess was locked firmly inside.

Everything seemed hopeless, until Passepartout had an idea...

The next morning, Princess Aouda was laid
beside her husband. Then the priests lit a huge
fire, watched by a silent crowd. Suddenly, the
air filled with screams. Some people even flung
themselves to the ground. The dead prince
was sitting up.

His ghostly figure rose through the smoke and grasped Princess Aouda in his arms. Then he strode off into the jungle.

"Let's go!" the ghost called to Fogg. It was Passepartout, who had disguised himself as the prince. Fogg and his friend chased after them, dodging bullets and arrows as they ran to safety.

Chapter 4
Tricked!

At Allahabad, Fogg gave the elephant to their
guide and jumped on a train. But Fix had
reported Passepartout's fight at the temple. As
they arrived in Calcutta, Fogg and Passepartout
were grabbed by police and taken to court.

Fogg and Passepartout faced a week in jail. The poor butler felt terrible. Then Fogg offered the court two thousand pounds.

"Very well," said the judge. "You may go free for now. But we'll keep the money if you don't return."

Fogg caught his next ship, to Hong Kong, with an hour to spare.

Fix was furious. "But Hong Kong belongs to Britain," he thought. "I can arrest Fogg there."

Princess Aouda, who hoped to find her cousin in Hong Kong, went too. When the ship stopped for coal in Singapore, Fogg and the princess went for a carriage ride.

They drove past pepper plants and nutmeg trees, grinning monkeys and grimacing tigers.

Near the end of the voyage, the ship battled against a raging wind. Fogg remained perfectly calm, but Passepartout was in a panic. "We'll miss our next ship, I know it!"

In the end, they reached Hong Kong one day late. Fogg had missed his next ship, which was to Yokohama in Japan.

"I knew it!" cried Passepartout.

Fix was delighted. "Now Fogg's stuck here and I can arrest him!" But luck was not on Fix's side.

It turned out that the ship to Yokohama had also been delayed, so Fogg hadn't missed it at all. Even worse, Fix's arrest papers *still* hadn't arrived.

Fix was desperate. Somehow, he had to keep Fogg in Hong Kong until the papers came.

Fogg booked a hotel for that night and set off to find Aouda's cousin. He sent Passepartout to reserve three cabins on their ship.

On the quay, Passepartout heard that the ship was sailing that very evening – and so did Fix.

"I must find my master!" the butler cried. But Fix invited him to a smoky inn for a drink first.

"I'm a detective and your master is a thief!" declared Fix, at the inn.

"Nonsense!" said Passepartout.

"Fogg mustn't know his ship sails tonight," thought Fix and bought the butler several more drinks. Before long, Passepartout was snoring and Fix had slipped away.

Fogg was on the quay early next morning and Princess Aouda was still with him. Her cousin had already left Hong Kong – and so, of course, had their ship. There was no sign of Passepartout either.

"I missed the ship too," said Fix.

The next steamer wasn't leaving for a week. But Fogg did not give up easily. Instead, he looked for another boat to take him to Japan.

Finally, Fogg found a captain of a small boat who agreed to take them to Shanghai. "You can catch another steamer for Yokohama from there," he said. Seeing Fix on the quay, Fogg offered him a lift.

Before the boat left, Fogg searched all over Hong Kong for Passepartout. But his butler had vanished.

For two days, the little boat sped through the waves. Then a great storm blew up and gigantic waves crashed upon the deck. The boat was tossed around on the sea like a ball.

When at last the wind dropped, they had lost
precious time. Even with all the sails hoisted,
the boat couldn't go fast enough.

Then Fogg spotted a steamer.

"That's the one from Shanghai to Yokohama,"
said the captain.

"Signal her," said Fogg.

With a bang, a rocket soared into the air and
the ship steamed over. As soon as it reached
them, Fogg, Aouda and Fix clambered aboard.

But, in the meantime, what had happened to Passepartout?

He had woken up just in time to catch the ship to Japan. Rushing on board at the last minute, he discovered – to his horror – that Fogg wasn't there.

When they landed at Yokohama, Passepartout didn't know what to do. He was wandering around in despair, when he saw a poster.

SEE THE FAMOUS ACROBATS - THE LONG NOSES!

LAST PERFORMANCE BEFORE THEY LEAVE FOR THE UNITED STATES!

"Maybe I could join the acrobats!" he said to himself. "They're going to America and that's where Fogg is heading next."

233

"Can you sing, standing on your head, with a top on your left foot and a sword on your right?" asked the owner of the group. Passepartout nodded. "You're in!"

That evening, he took part in his first show, at the bottom of a human triangle. The crowd loved it. But suddenly...

all the acrobats
collapsed

in a heap.

Passepartout had spotted
Phileas Fogg, jumped up and run over.

Chapter 5
Racing home

They had no time for explanations. Fogg and his beaming butler raced to catch their next ship, for San Francisco. Princess Aouda, who had nowhere else to go, came too. She grew fonder of Fogg each day.

236

As the ship steamed on, Passepartout began to think Fogg would win his bet. But one day he saw Fix on deck. The inspector had secretly followed them.

Passepartout hit him.

"Wait!" cried Fix. "It might have seemed I was against you before..."

"You were!" said Passepartout.

"Well, yes," agreed Fix, "and I still think Fogg's a thief. But now I want him in England. It's only in England I can arrest him."

237

Passepartout didn't want to worry Fogg, so he kept quiet about Fix. But when Fogg went to get his passport stamped in San Francisco, he bumped into the inspector too.

"What a surprise!" lied Fix and joined them on the next stage of the journey, crossing America by train.

The Pacific Railroad steamed right across the country to New York. It had every luxury on board, from shops to restaurants, but it still had to wait when a herd of buffalo crossed the track.

238

The next obstacle was a shaky bridge. "I'll cross at top speed!" said the driver. He went so fast the wheels barely touched the tracks.

The train reared up and jumped across. As it landed on the other side, the bridge crashed into the river.

Soon after that, they hit real trouble. The train was steaming by some rocky cliffs, when a band of Sioux warriors jumped onto its roof. The warriors quickly took over driving the train. "There is a fort near the next station," shouted a guard. "If only we could stop the train."

Passepartout sped into action.

Crawling under the train, he wriggled and swung all the way to the engine, without being seen.

Then, he unhooked the engine and the train slowly came to a halt... just beside the station.

But when Fogg looked for his butler a few seconds later, he'd gone.

"The warriors took him when they fled!" shouted a guard.

Calling over some soldiers, Fogg went into the hills to look for him.

It took all day to find and free Passepartout. They had to camp out overnight and only got back to the station the following morning.

By then, their train had long since left and the next one wasn't due until that evening.

"I've done it again," wailed the butler. But Fix came to the rescue.

"I've just met a man who owns a land yacht," he announced.

Soon, they were gliding over the snow. Wind filled the yacht's sails and it whizzed over the icy plains.

They caught up with the train for New York at the very next station. It puffed across the country at top speed. Fogg still had a chance.

They finally stopped at a station by the steamship pier, on the bank of the River Hudson in New York. But the ship to England had already left – it had sailed just forty-five minutes earlier.

No other steamers could take them across the Atlantic Ocean in time. Passepartout was crushed, but Fogg visited every ship in the port. Once again, he found a captain who would take passengers.

The ship was sailing to France, but that didn't worry Fogg. He simply locked the captain in his cabin and changed course.

The ship was fast, but it was now winter and the weather was terrible. Then the engineer gave Fogg more bad news.

"The coal for the boiler is running out!" he said grimly.

"Even my clever master can't solve this," thought Passepartout.

Once again, Fogg surprised him. He ordered the sailors to cut down the mast and chop it into logs.

Then he told the astonished men to burn the wood in the ship's boiler.

Over the next three days, the sailors burned the ship's bridge...

the
cabins...

and even the decks.

By the time they reached England, only the ship's metal hull was left.

They landed in Liverpool, with just enough time for Fogg to catch a train to London and win his bet. But, as Fogg stepped off the ship, Fix made his move.

"Phileas Fogg," the detective announced, "I arrest you for stealing fifty-five thousand pounds."

Fogg was thrown into prison and there was absolutely nothing Princess Aouda or Passepartout could do.

Three hours later, they were waiting for news, when Fix rushed in. His hair was a mess and he looked ashamed.

"I've made a dreadful mistake," he cried. "The real thief was arrested three days ago!"

Fogg was free again. But he had only five and a half hours left.

Fogg, calm as ever, paid for a special train which roared down to London. As it pulled in, he checked the station clock – 8:55. Fogg had lost his bet by just ten minutes.

"I can't believe it," Passepartout cried.

"We came so close."

Chapter 6
What next?

Phileas Fogg did not show any sign of how
he felt. He simply left the station with
Passepartout and Aouda and drove home. The
next day, he stayed in his room, adding up all
the money he had lost.

At seven o'clock, Fogg visited Princess Aouda in her room.

"Madam," he said sadly, "When I brought you to England, I planned to give you a fortune. But I am afraid now it is not possible."

"My dear sir," the princess replied gently, "I don't want your money... just you."

"You want to marry me?" He couldn't believe what he was hearing.

Fogg was overjoyed and, for the first time in his life, it showed. "Passepartout!" he called. "Run to the church and book our wedding for tomorrow!"

"On a Monday?" Passepartout asked.

"On a Monday," Fogg laughed.

Meanwhile Fogg's friends at his club had spent the last few days in a fever of excitement. They had not heard a word from Fogg since he left on October 2nd.

On the evening of December 21st, they waited eagerly to see if he would show. And, as the hands on the clock reached 8:44, they heard a knock on the door.

It was Phileas Fogg in person. But how had he done it? Well, Passepartout had returned from the priest with incredible news.

"Not Monday tomorrow," he gasped. "Tomorrow, Sunday. Today is... SATURDAY!"

Going around the world to the east had gained Fogg an extra day. He'd had ten minutes left to get to the club and win his bet.

Fogg won twenty thousand pounds but, as he had spent nearly nineteen thousand pounds on the way, he wasn't much better off.

On the other hand, he did find a wife and happiness on his trip. Most people would go around the world for less!

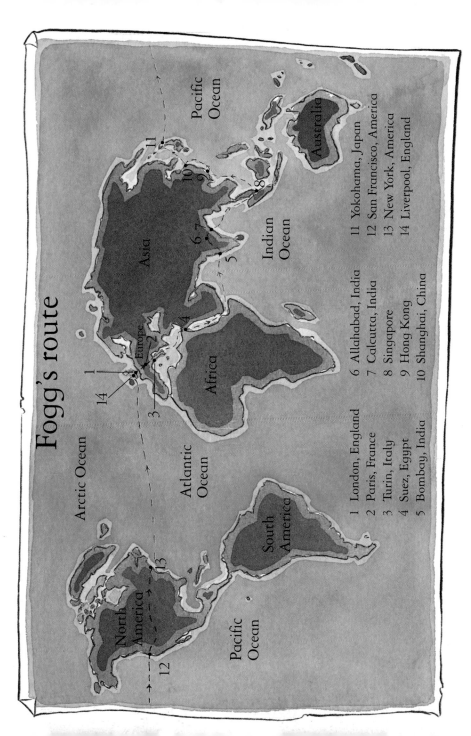

Fogg's route

Arctic Ocean

Atlantic Ocean

Pacific Ocean

Pacific Ocean

Indian Ocean

Europe

Asia

Africa

North America

South America

Australia

1 London, England
2 Paris, France
3 Turin, Italy
4 Suez, Egypt
5 Bombay, India
6 Allahabad, India
7 Calcutta, India
8 Singapore
9 Hong Kong
10 Shanghai, China
11 Yokohama, Japan
12 San Francisco, America
13 New York, America
14 Liverpool, England

Robinson Crusoe

Daniel Defoe (1659-1731)

Daniel Defoe was an English writer, journalist and spy. He wrote hundreds of books in his lifetime on all sorts of subjects. Defoe was born in London, and when he was young witnessed two of the most dramatic events of the time – the Great Plague and the Great Fire of London. *Robinson Crusoe*, the novel he is best known for, was first published in 1719. It was based on the real life adventure of Alexander Selkirk.

Chapter 1
Shipwreck!

Long ago, there lived a boy called Robinson
Crusoe. He wasn't at all interested in school, or
books. All he could think about was being
a sailor.

As soon as he was old enough, he set off on his travels. A few years later, some of his friends planned a trip to Africa, and asked him to go with them.

Crusoe eagerly agreed and, soon after that, the men set sail.

All went well until a storm blew up. Huge waves crashed into the masts and ripped the sails. Then there was a sickening crunch. "We've hit a sandbank!" cried one of the men. They were forced to abandon ship.

But the storm was too much for their little
boat. It was tossed around in the heaving sea.
Then, suddenly, a gigantic wave tipped it
right over.

Robinson Crusoe felt himself sinking.
Desperately, he began to swim for the shore.

After battling through the waves, he reached land. When at last he finally got his breath back, he emptied his pockets.

He had a knife, his pipe and some tobacco. That was it. How ever was he going to survive?

Chapter 2
The island home

The next day, when the storm had died down, Crusoe looked for his friends. All he could find were shoes and a hat. He was totally alone. "What will I do?" he wondered.

He decided to
see what he could
find on the ship. It
was easy to reach,
now the water was
calm. He found a
rope hanging down
and hauled himself
aboard.

He was so hungry,
he headed straight for
the storeroom. To
his delight, he found
that the food was still
dry. So he stuffed his
pockets with it, and
went about examining
the rest of the ship.

"I know!" he thought. "I'll make a raft to carry things back to shore."

First, he tied four poles together. With pieces of wood fixed across them, the raft was strong enough to stand on.

Crusoe found lots of useful things on the wrecked ship: chests of food, barrels of rum, gunpowder and guns. He loaded up the raft with as much as it would hold and paddled back to the beach.

Crusoe sailed to and fro on his raft, rescuing tools, clothes, plenty of wood and some sails.

On one trip, he heard a strange noise. Was it a bark? He looked around the ship. Suddenly, the ship's dog bounded up to him, followed by the ship's two cats.

Crusoe was delighted. He wasn't completely alone after all.

Soon, Crusoe had enough things to make
a home. He found a sheltered spot by a cliff,
looking out to sea.

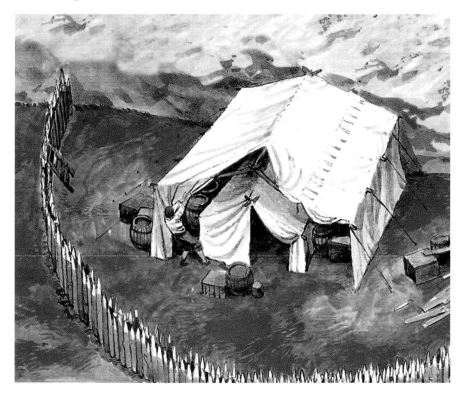

Using the ship's sails, he built a tent. Then he
built a bigger tent over the top of it, to protect it
from the rain.

271

At the back of the tent, there was a sandy cave.

"If I made the cave bigger, I could use it as a storeroom," Crusoe thought. But he didn't have a shovel...

"I'll make one out of wood!" he decided.

He dug out some earth and sand. Soon, the cave was much bigger. Pleased with his wooden spade, he made shelves, a table and a chair.

Chapter 3
A new way of life

Crusoe soon got used to life on the island.
Every morning, he went hunting with his dog.
He shot birds and wild goats for food.

274

Sometimes, he clambered over the cliffs, looking for birds' eggs to cook for breakfast.

One day, while he was out exploring, he made an exciting discovery: ripe ears of corn. He picked them and kept the grain to sow in the spring.
"Now I'll be able to make bread!" he thought.

Every lunchtime, he went home and cooked his food over a fire.

He skinned the animals he shot, and dried their skins to use later.

The afternoons were very hot, much too hot to work.

So, after lunch, Crusoe climbed into a hammock he'd made and snoozed.

276

After his nap, Crusoe stayed near his tent, making things. When it got dark, he wrote a diary by candlelight.

I came on shore here on the 30th September 1659

Time passed quickly. So he wouldn't lose track of it, he made notches on a pole, one notch every day and a bigger notch on Sundays.

Crusoe explored every part of the island.
There was a beautiful valley in the middle,
where orange trees grew...

...there were melons growing
on the ground and
lots of wonderful
vines, with rich
crops of grapes.
It was a paradise.

Crusoe began to make friends with the animals, too. He spent hours teaching a young parrot to speak.

One day, he accidentally shot a baby goat. He took it home to nurse and, before long, it became tame.

Just before the rains came, he planted his grains of corn. The corn grew fast and soon he had a fine cornfield.

But there was a problem. Most of the birds thought the corn looked good, too.

Crusoe had to fire his gun into the air, to scare them away.

Crusoe wondered what he should store the corn in. Finally, he decided to make some clay pots.

It wasn't easy. His first pots had very wobbly edges. But Crusoe soon got better at making them. He left the pots to dry in the sun and then baked them in a fire.

Finally, the corn was ready to bake. First, Crusoe ground it down into flour, using a piece of wood he'd carved. Then he mixed it with some water.

He shaped the mixture into round loaves and cooked them on a tile over a fire of hot ashes.

Chapter 4
Stuck forever?

One morning, Crusoe walked to a different part of the island. Looking out to sea he saw land, far away. Suddenly, he felt very alone.

"I'll escape!" he decided. "I'll make myself a boat and escape."

So he cut down a big tree and chopped off all the branches. Then he began to hollow out the trunk.

After weeks of hard work, the boat was finished. Crusoe looked at it thoughtfully. It was huge.

284

When he tried to push the heavy boat down to the sea, it wouldn't budge. He shoved... and he heaved... It was no good.

"I'll have to dig a canal from the boat," he realized. "Then I can float it to the water."

But that didn't work either. It was just too much for one man to do. "I'm stuck," thought Crusoe sadly.

He sighed. He'd been on the island for four long years and his clothes were in rags.

"If I'm going to stay, I'd better make myself some new clothes," he said.

Taking pieces of goatskin, he sewed himself a new pair of breeches, a jacket and a hat.

286

Proudly, he tried them on. His new clothes probably looked odd, but Crusoe was delighted.

To complete his new outfit, he made an umbrella out of sticks and covered it with goatskin.

Now, he stayed dry when it rained. The umbrella protected him from the fierce sun as well.

"I think I'll build another home," Crusoe decided. "A lovely summer house in the valley where the orange trees grow."

So he built a tent in the valley and planted trees around it. It was a perfect place to relax in the hot summer months.

One day, Crusoe thought, "Since this island's my home, I ought to get to know it as well as I can. I think I'll explore the coast." And he made another boat.

The second boat was far too small to escape in, but it was ideal for sailing around the island. So off he went.

On his return, he made a map and marked all the places he had discovered. He realized that he didn't mind staying on the island after all.

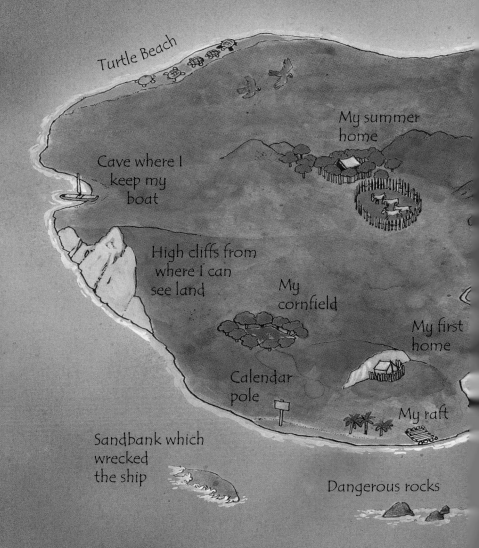

Turtle Beach

My summer home

Cave where I keep my boat

High cliffs from where I can see land

My cornfield

My first home

Calendar pole

My raft

Sandbank which wrecked the ship

Dangerous rocks

"I'm king of the island now!" he said to himself. He had everything he needed and he was perfectly happy. The years flew past.

Lemon trees

Rocky Point

Lookout point

The first boat I made

The cliff I climbed when I arrived

N
W ← → E
S

Chapter 5
Visitors

But then everything changed. One day, Crusoe
was wandering along the beach when he saw
a footprint. He stared at it for a moment, his
heart thumping, then ran home.

Crusoe was so scared, he hid for a week. Finally, he shook himself. "This is silly!" he thought. "It's probably my own footprint!"

So, he went back and measured his foot against the print. But the footprint was larger. It definitely belonged to someone else.

The footprint made Crusoe very nervous. But days, weeks, months passed and no one came... until the afternoon he was out hunting, when he made a grim discovery.

On the beach were the remains of a fire and human bones. Crusoe felt sick. Something terrible had happened here.

He didn't feel happy on the island any more. Every day, he watched the sea anxiously. Maybe the visitor would come back.

For several months, he waited. Again, nothing happened. Then, early one morning, he spotted a fire on the beach.

He crept closer to watch. From his hiding place, he saw a group of people dancing around a fire and feasting.

Watching them, Crusoe felt uneasy. When their party came to an end, the people jumped into their canoes and paddled away.

Now, Crusoe was very worried. He had the feeling they wouldn't like him to be on the island. "They may find me someday," he said to himself. "I'd better be ready."

So he strengthened the fence around his home and fixed guns into it. Then he planted trees around the fence to hide that. He wasn't taking any chances.

Chapter 6
The captive

Another two years went by, with no sign of
the visitors. Then, one summer's day, Crusoe
spotted five canoes, packed with people and
nearing the beach. He crept closer.

The men landed, built a huge fire and began
to roast chunks of meat on it. They had two
captives with them.

As Crusoe watched, the men hit one of the
captives over the head.

Suddenly, the other captive broke away from the group and started to run. Two of the men chased after him.

Crusoe gasped.

"Those men will kill him if they recapture him," Crusoe thought. "He could be my friend! I'll try to help."

He followed the men until the main group was out of sight. Then he jumped out and hit one of the pair with his gun.

The other man raised his bow, but Crusoe was too quick for him. He fired his gun and the man fell.

The captive stopped running, rooted to the spot with fear. Crusoe could see that he was trembling. He smiled, to show that he was friendly and beckoned to him.

The man smiled back. He followed Crusoe home and they had a large meal of bread and raisins.

After that, the man gave a huge yawn. Soon, he was fast asleep.

The next day, Crusoe tried talking with his new friend. It was difficult, because he didn't speak English. Crusoe started by giving the man an English name.

"I'll call you Friday," he said, "after the day we met."

Friday didn't have any clothes with him, so Crusoe gave him some of his. Friday wasn't sure what to make of them. Crusoe's clothes had a style all of their own.

Crusoe was delighted. Now, he had a friend to hunt and farm with. Friday was happy to share the cooking too, and helped Crusoe to grind corn and make bread.

Crusoe couldn't speak Friday's language, but Friday began to pick up English quickly.

Crusoe was very happy. It was good to have someone to talk to at last.

One day, they climbed the cliff and Friday spotted the mainland. He was very excited. "That's my home!" he cried. "Let's make a boat and go there."

"Will your friends like me?" asked Crusoe.

"Of course!" said Friday.

Crusoe's huge boat had rotted, so they built a new one and began to gather food for their journey. But before they were ready, disaster struck. Friday saw three canoes sailing to the island.

He ran to tell Crusoe. Their plans would have to wait...

Chapter 7
Battle

Crusoe and Friday loaded their guns and hid.
As they watched, the visitors danced around
a captive on the beach. Crusoe raised his gun.
"Fire!" he shouted to Friday.

The men panicked. They fled to their canoes, while Friday kept shooting.

Crusoe ran to the captive, a sailor, and quickly untied him. Thrusting a gun in his hand, Crusoe told him that he would have to defend himself.

The battle was soon over. All the visitors escaped, but they left two canoes behind. Crusoe and Friday were all set to chase after them in a canoe, when Crusoe looked inside one of them and gasped. An old man was lying in the bottom of the boat, tied up.

Crusoe helped the old man out of the boat.
As he untied him, Friday shouted with joy.
   "It's my father!" he cried.
   He rushed up to the old man and hugged him.

Friday and Crusoe took the captives home.
They gave them a good meal and let them rest.
    Later, the sailor told Crusoe that his friends
were still on the mainland.

Crusoe gave the sailor food and weapons
and the man left, agreeing to take Friday's
father home.

Chapter 8
Escape at last?

Only a week later, Crusoe saw a ship moored close to the island... an English ship! He could hardly believe it, another ship after so long.

Feeling excited, he fetched his telescope. A small boat was coming ashore, full of sailors. But three of them had their hands tied.

The sailors took their prisoners to a tree and tied them up. Then they wandered off along the beach.

Friday and Crusoe waited a while, to make sure the others had gone. Finally, they went down to the beach to see what was going on.

The prisoners stared at Crusoe. Then one of them spoke. "I'm the captain of that ship," he said. "My sailors mutinied. Some of them rowed us to this island to leave us here to die."

"That's terrible!" said Crusoe. Then he smiled. He'd had an idea. "Well, we'll help you to escape..." he began, "...if you promise to take us to England."

The captain nodded. "Of course," he agreed eagerly.

When the sailors came back from exploring the island, they had a shock. Crusoe, Friday and the prisoners jumped out from behind some bushes and seized them. They stood no chance.

"We'll spare your lives if you help us," said Crusoe.

The sailors agreed. They didn't really have much choice.

Later that night, the captain rowed out to
the ship with the few men he could trust. They
crept aboard very quietly... and opened fire.

The rebels were taken by surprise and
panicked.

"Stop! We surrender!" they cried. "You can
have your ship back."

The next day, the captain rowed back to shore.

"Come aboard!" he told Crusoe. "We leave for England today!"

On board the ship, Crusoe put on his first English clothes for many years. Friday laughed when he saw them.

Friday had decided to sail for England too. Crusoe took one last look at the island that had been his home for thirty-five years. Then the sailors hauled in the anchor and the ship set sail.

Friday and Crusoe stayed friends for the rest of their lives. Both loved their life in England, but they never forgot their time on the island together.

The Canterville Ghost

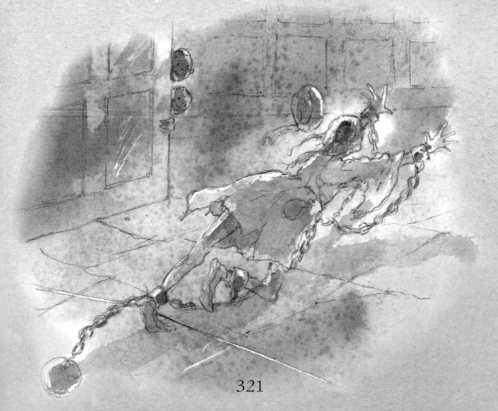

Oscar Wilde (1854-1900)

The writer Oscar Wilde was born in Ireland, but
moved to London when he was 24. His first
book, *Poems*, was published in 1881.
The Canterville Ghost was written in
1887. Wilde also wrote fairy tales for
his two sons, but he is best known
for his plays, which are still
performed today.

Chapter 1
Canterville Castle

Mr. Otis looked at the castle with delight. "I'll buy it!" he cried.

"Excellent," replied his guide, Lord Canterville. "But perhaps I should warn you... Canterville Castle is haunted."

"My family had to move out many years ago, after my great-aunt had a dreadful experience."

"She saw a skeleton. She never recovered."

Mr. Otis wasn't worried. He didn't believe in ghosts. "I'm sure my family and I will be very happy here," he smiled.

325

A week later, Mr. and Mrs. Otis arrived with their children, Washington, Virginia and the twins. They were greeted by an old woman, who was neatly dressed in a white apron and cap.

"I'm Mrs. Umney, the housekeeper," she said. "Come inside. There's tea for you in the library."

326

"Cake!" shouted the twins, diving in. Virginia wasn't interested in the food. She had spotted a poem in the library window.

If a child will enter the secret room
And stay till the dead of the night
Then at last Sir Simon can sleep in his tomb
And at Canterville all will be right.

Before she could show her father, Mrs. Otis cried out. "Oh dear! I'm afraid we've spilled something on the carpet, Mrs. Umney."

327

"It wasn't you madam," replied Mrs. Umney in a hushed voice. "*Blood* has been spilled there."

"How horrible!" cried Mrs. Otis. "It must be removed at once."

Mrs. Umney looked around nervously and began to speak in a low voice.

"It is the blood of Lady Eleanor Canterville. She was murdered on that very spot by her husband, Sir Simon Canterville, five hundred years ago."

"Seven years later, Sir Simon Canterville disappeared. His body has never been found."

Mrs. Umney's voice began to shake. "His spirit haunts this house. That blood stain will never go."

Washington jumped down onto the carpet and scrubbed at the blood stain. Within seconds, it was gone.

But as he stood up there was a crash of
thunder and a terrible flash of lightning.

Mrs. Umney fainted.

The thunderstorm lasted the entire night.
Rain lashed at the windows and the wind
howled down the chimneys.

And next morning, in the very same spot on the library carpet, there was the blood stain.

Chapter 2
Clanking chains

"There must be a simple explanation," cried Mr. Otis.

That night, Mr. Otis locked the library door himself and took the key to bed with him. But the blood stain still came back.

After what happened the following night, Mr. Otis thought differently about ghosts.

At midnight, he was woken by a strange noise outside his room.

It sounded like rusty chains being dragged along the ground and it seemed to be coming closer every second.

Mr. Otis was annoyed. He put on his slippers and picked up a small bottle from his bedside table. Then he opened the door...

...to a terrible sight. An old
man, with long greasy hair
and ragged clothes was
glaring at him out of
fiery red eyes.

"You must be Sir Simon," said Mr. Otis calmly. "I'm afraid, my dear sir, I must ask you to oil your chains. They make an awful noise. This bottle of oil should help."

Mr. Otis left the bottle on a table and went back to bed.

For a moment the Canterville Ghost was still. Then he smashed the bottle of oil onto the floor and fled down the corridor, howling.

The twins heard him. As Sir Simon reached the top of the stairs, they raced out of their bedroom with a pillow. Sir Simon felt a rush of air as the pillow whizzed past his head. It very nearly hit him.

The ghost quickly vanished, to appear in
his secret chamber in the west wing. He
was furious.

"I have been scaring people for hundreds
of years," he grumbled, "but never have
I been treated like this."

"How dare these newcomers give me oil for
my chains and throw pillows at my head. I must
get my revenge!"

Chapter 3
The ghost's revenge

"There's no
need to be scared
of ghosts," Mr. Otis told his family
the next morning, "but you mustn't throw
pillows at them. It's rude."

The twins grinned.

"We'll have to take those chains off him," said Mrs. Otis, "or we'll never get any sleep." But for the rest of that week there was no sign of the ghost.

The twins looked for him everywhere. They wanted to play more tricks on him.

Fresh blood stains continued to appear each morning. Strangely, each stain was a different shade. The family made guesses as to what shade it would be next.

One morning, it was even a brilliant green. When she saw that, Virginia looked cross, though she wouldn't say why.

Meanwhile, the ghost was busy plotting his revenge. He spent days looking over his wardrobe, deciding what to wear.

He planned to creep to Washington's room and make faces at the boy from the foot of his bed. Then, he would stab himself in the neck three times to the sound of slow music.

Sir Simon especially disliked Washington. It was Washington who kept removing the blood stains.

Virginia, on the other hand, had never been rude. "I shall only groan at her a few times from her wardrobe," he thought. "As for the twins..."

The twins, of course, deserved the worst treatment. He'd get them. He would turn into a skeleton and crawl around their beds, staring at them from one rolling eyeball.

At half-past ten the family went to bed. For a while Sir Simon heard shrieks of laughter from the twins' room, but at last all was quiet.

He crept stealthily into the corridor. An owl beat its wings against the window pane, but the Otis family slept on, peacefully unaware.

Sir Simon glided along like an evil shadow,
a cruel smile stretching his wrinkled mouth.
Finally, he reached the corner of the passage
that led to Washington's room.

He chuckled to himself, turned the corner,
then let out a wail of terror. Sir Simon fell back,
hiding his face in his bony white hands.

Right in front of him was a horrible vision.
It was bald and white, with red light
streaming from its eyes. Sir Simon
had never seen another ghost
before. He was terrified.

He fled back to his room, tripping on his
sheet as he went.

Back in his chamber, he flung himself into his coffin and slammed down the lid. But as the sun rose, his bravery returned.

"I shall go and talk to the ghost," he decided. "Perhaps we can deal with the twins together. Two ghosts have got to be better than one."

By morning, the ghost looked very different. The light had gone from its eyes and it had collapsed against the wall.

Sir Simon rushed forward and seized it in his arms. To his horror, its head slipped off and rolled on the floor.

He was holding a white curtain, a broom and a large pumpkin. He had been tricked! Sir Simon ground his toothless gums together in fury, swore revenge and stomped back to his coffin.

Chapter 4
Sir Simon is upset

Sir Simon was cross and tired. The excitement of the past few days had been too much for him. For five days he stayed in his room. He even gave up making new blood stains.

With the twins constantly playing tricks on him, he only felt safe in his room. He knew it was his ghostly duty to appear in the corridor once a week, but he made sure he wasn't seen or heard.

He even slipped into Mr. Otis's bedroom and took a bottle of oil for his chains. But he still wasn't left alone.

The twins put down pins for him to tread on. One night they even stretched a piece of string across the corridor.

"That's it!" he decided. "I'm going to scare those twins one last time, if it kills me."

353

"I'll appear as my most terrifying character, Reckless Rupert the Headless Earl," he thought. Reckless Rupert always worked.

Sir Simon spent two days getting ready. Finally, he was satisfied with his appearance.

As the clock struck midnight, he made his way to the twins' bedroom. He flung open the door...

...and a large jug of icy water tipped over him. He was soaked. Sir Simon heard muffled shrieks of laughter from the twins' beds.

Furious, Sir Simon squelched back to his room. The next day he had a very bad cold. "I must give up all hope of scaring the Otis family," he said sadly.

He started creeping along the passages in his slippers.

One night he decided to creep to the library. He wanted to see if there was any blood left on the carpet. Suddenly, two figures jumped out at him from the darkness.

In terror, Sir Simon ran to the stairs. But there was Washington Otis, aiming a garden hose at him.

Chapter 5
The secret chamber

Some weeks later, Virginia was out walking in the fields, when she tore her dress climbing through a hedge.

"I'll have to change," she thought, and decided to go up the back staircase, so she wouldn't be seen. On the way, she noticed that the door to the Tapestry Room was open.

"How odd!" she thought. "No one ever uses the Tapestry Room." Virginia peered around the door. To her surprise, she saw the Canterville Ghost.

Sir Simon was sitting by the window, his head in his hands. He looked so upset Virginia thought she should try and comfort him.

"Cheer up," she said. "The boys are going to school tomorrow, so the tricks will stop. Besides, if you behave yourself, no one will annoy you."

Sir Simon jumped up. "How can I behave myself?" he shouted. "I have to rattle my chains and groan through keyholes and walk around at night. I'm a ghost."

"You don't *have* to do anything," said Virginia.
"What's more, you've been very wicked. Mrs.
Umney told us that you murdered your wife.
It's wrong to kill people,"
she pointed out.

"Yes, it was wrong," sighed Sir Simon, "but
that was no reason for her brothers to starve me
to death."

"Oh, poor ghost!" said Virginia. "I didn't know about that. Are you hungry now? Would you like a sandwich?"

"No thank you," he answered. "I never eat now. But it's kind of you to offer. You know," he added, "you're much nicer than the rest of your horrible family."

"How dare you be rude about my family!" cried Virginia. "You're mean, you lie and you stole all the paints out of my paint box for that blood stain. First my reds, then the yellows – even the greens."

"I think you should apologize," Virginia demanded, angrily.

The ghost shrugged. "I don't see why I should. After all, what else could I do? Real blood is so hard to get hold of these days. And your brother would keep cleaning up."

"Fine," said Virginia. "If you won't apologize, I'm leaving." She turned to go.

"No, don't go," the ghost cried out.

"Please help me," Sir Simon called. "I'm so unhappy and so very, very tired."

Now Virginia was curious. "Why are you tired? Can't you sleep?"

"I haven't slept for five hundred years," Sir Simon told her.

Virginia gasped.

"And it would be so pleasant to lie in the soft brown earth," the ghost went on, "with grasses waving above my head, listening to silence..."

"Can't anyone help you?" asked Virginia.

"You could," whispered the ghost.

Virginia trembled as he spoke and a cold shudder passed through her. "How?" she asked.

"Have you ever read the poem on the library window?"

"Yes, often." Virginia thought of it now.

> If a child will enter the secret room
> And stay till the dead of the night
> Then at last Sir Simon can sleep in his tomb
> And at Canterville all will be right.

"But I don't know what it means."

"It means," said the ghost, "that you must come with me to my secret chamber and pray for me."

"That sounds easy," said Virginia.

"Mmm," said Sir Simon, "but no living person has ever entered the chamber and come out alive."

Virginia was terrified. But she did want to help. "I'll come with you, Sir Simon," she said bravely. "Lead the way."

Sir Simon took her hand in his cold, clammy
fingers. Together they walked to the end of
the room, where the wall disappeared before
her eyes.

In a moment, the wall had closed behind
them and Virginia vanished into the ghost's
secret chamber.

Chapter 6

Peace at last

Ten minutes later the bell rang for tea. As Virginia did not appear, Mrs. Otis sent a footman to find her. But the footman couldn't find her anywhere.

At first Mrs. Otis thought she must be in the stables. When Virginia still hadn't returned two hours later, she began to panic.

"Boys," she called to her sons, "go and see if you can find her." But she was nowhere to be found.

Mrs. Otis even asked Mr. Otis to drain the fish pond. But there was no sign of Virginia anywhere.

At last the family sat down to supper. It was a sad meal and hardly anyone spoke. Even the twins were quiet. As the family left the dining room, the clock in the tower began to strike midnight.

On the last stroke there was a crash and a sudden, shrill cry. A panel at the top of the staircase flew back and Virginia staggered out.

Everyone rushed up to her. Mrs. Otis hugged her, Mr. Otis patted her head and the twins danced around them all.

"Where have you been?" said Mrs. Otis, rather angrily. "I've been so worried. You must not play tricks, Virginia."

"I've been with the ghost," said Virginia
quietly. "He's gone. He's been very wicked, but
he was sorry for everything he'd done. And
look! He gave me this box of jewels just before
he left."

Four days later, they held a funeral for Sir Simon. The procession left Canterville Castle at eleven o'clock at night. The carriages were drawn by four black horses, each with a great tuft of ostrich-feathers on its head.

Lord Canterville came all the way from
Wales to take part. He sat in the first carriage
with Virginia. Then came Mr. and Mrs. Otis,
followed by Washington and the twins.

It was all wonderfully impressive.

379

In the last carriage sat Mrs. Umney. After all, she had been frightened of the ghost for fifty years. It was only fair she should see the last of him.

The next day Mr. Otis had a word with Lord Canterville. "I think we should return the box of jewels to you. They're beautiful. Especially the ruby necklace."

"No thank you, Mr. Otis," replied Lord Canterville. "The jewels were given to Virginia for being so brave and I think she truly deserves them."

Virginia wore the ruby necklace whenever she went to a party. But, however much Washington and the twins begged, she never told anyone what happened in the secret chamber.

And Sir Simon lay in peace, at last sleeping beneath the soft earth.

Sir Simon
Canterville

R.I.P.

Edited by Rachel Firth and Lesley Sims

Designed by Caroline Spatz

Additional design by Emily Bornoff and Michelle Lawrence

Cover Design: Zoe Wray

First published in 2008 by Usborne Publishing Ltd, 83-85 Saffron Hill,
London EC1N 8RT, England.
www.usborne.com Copyright © 2008 Usborne Publishing Ltd.
First published in America in 2010. UE.